GIRLS ARE SUPER STRONG

Exciting and Motivational Stories for Girls about Confidence, Self Love and Mindfulness

David Wilson

ISBN – 9798757755311

This book belongs to

....

....

Contents

Tim the elephant

Tim was a cute little elephant. He had a big mummy and a giant daddy, and he also had something that made him special.

Tim had the biggest, kindest heart of any elephant in the village. Everywhere he went, he tried to make people happy. It made him smile when he gave people something they liked. That was why Tim always took extra snacks with him wherever he went.

One day, Tim was walking home from school. He saw a little bear crying by the side of the road. When he went up to her, he knew something was wrong. The little bear had a thorn in her paw, and it was hurting her. What could Tim do? He made it his mission to make her smile!

He walked over to her, smiled, and offered her one of his snacks. It was a big cream cake that made her eyes light up the moment she saw it. She smiled back, reached out and grabbed the cake, and sank her teeth into it. She didn't even notice Tim sucking the thorn out of her paw with his mighty trunk.

When she'd finished licking her lips, she looked at Tim and smiled. He knew he'd made her happy and that she felt better. It was the best feeling in the world. He gave her a big hug and carried on his way.

Around the next corner, Tim saw a snake that was hissing with fury. He walked up to him and saw that the snake had tied himself in a knot. He'd never seen anything quite like it!

When he reached out his trunk to try to help, the snake hissed even louder. He was angry and didn't want anyone to come near him. Tim reached into his bag with his trunk, took out a big bag of crunchy crisps, and gave them to the snake. In the blink of an eye, the snake was quietly eating the crisps. Tim knew exactly what to do next.

While the snake was happily eating, he got to work untying the knot. Before he knew it, the snake was back to his old self. He gave Tim a big smile. Tim gave him a little tickle with his trunk, let him keep the rest of the crisps, and carried on walking.

It was getting hot, so Tim walked down to the river to cool himself down. He splashed water everywhere with his trunk and had a jolly old time. When he got out of the water to have a rest and some lunch, he heard someone coughing. Who could it be?

Nearby, he saw a big carp, coughing like nothing he had ever heard before. He was stuck on the river bank and needed to get back in the water. Tim sprung into action straight away and picked him up with his trunk. The carp took a big deep breath the moment he hit the water, then smiled wider than ever before.

The carp didn't want a snack from Tim; he said that his kind act was all he could have ever wished for. In return, he told Tim about a big apple tree on the other side of the river that he saw every time he swam past it. Tim had done something kind for him, so he wanted to do something to make Tim smile too.

Once the carp had swum away down the river, Tim dried himself off in the sunshine and started thinking about all those juicy apples. How crunchy would they be? How sweet would they be? How much fun he was going to have picking them all!

He picked up his things, filled up his bag, and set off for the other side of the river. It was going to be quite an adventure! Soon, Tim got to the apple tree, but that wasn't all he found. A little girl was picking up all the fallen apples and putting them in her basket. She told Tim she needed to take them home so her parents could cook, but so many of the apples on the ground had been eaten by worms.

Tim was big and tall; the girl was small and clever. She told Tim that if he reached down the best apples, he could keep half and she could keep the other half. But couldn't Tim just keep all the apples for himself?

He thought about it for a moment, then realised what the girl had known all along.

Tim's bag was nearly full because he took snacks with him wherever he went. If he wanted to take plenty of apples, he'd have to leave the snacks behind.

The little girl went behind the tree and pulled out a spare bag. She gave it to Tim, and he smiled. The girl was sharing her bag so Tim would help fetch the apples for her. If they worked together, they'd each be able to take more apples home than they would by themselves.

They spent hours talking, telling jokes, and sharing some of Tim's snacks. By sunset, they each had a mountain of the freshest, juiciest apples they had ever seen. Tim picked up his apples and was about to wave goodbye when he saw the girl struggling. Her apples were far too heavy!

He picked her up with his trunk and put her on his back. He said that he would take his new friend all the way home so she wouldn't have to leave a single apple behind.

And do you know the best bit for Tim?

The little girl promised to show him where he could find the sweetest, tastiest blackberries he'd ever tried.

Being kind was Tim's superpower. It made him happy, made people smile, and made it easy to make lots of new friends.

The courageous little girl

Lucy was the smallest girl in her class. She was tiny!

She had the smallest feet and the smallest hands. You could barely see her in the playground when everyone was running about.

Lucy knew she was small and she never let it bother her. One day, she would grow big and strong like all her friends, so for now, she enjoyed being small.

She could climb trees no one else could climb. She could fit into hiding places where no one else could find her. And she could beat anyone in a game of tag because she was so hard to catch. There was so much she liked about being small.

One day, Lucy came into her class and saw a new girl waiting at the front with the teacher.

She was the tallest girl Lucy had ever seen, and everyone was looking at her.

They were all whispering about how old she must be. Surely she wasn't in the same class as they all were. But none of this bothered Lucy. All she wanted was to make a new friend.

When the girl had finished speaking to the teacher, she looked around the classroom for a place to sit. Everyone was avoiding looking at her and pretending to be busy with their friends, except Lucy.

She waved at the girl, smiled, and invited her to come and take a seat. The new girl was a little nervous, but that didn't stop Lucy from wanting to make friends with her. She even moved her bag and her pencil case so her new classmate could sit down; her name was Karen.

Karen wasn't sure what to do when she sat down, so Lucy just gave her a smile and told her a joke. She even managed to get a little smile to appear on Karen's freckly face.

They worked together on the maths problems the teacher was writing on the board, and Karen amazed Lucy with how good she was with numbers. For a moment, Lucy thought the only way she could be so good was if she really was much older, but then she remembered something...

Lucy was never bothered about being small, but she knew people who would be. She didn't know Karen very well yet, but what if she was shy about being so tall? Lucy knew she had to be kind to Karen and let her come out of her shell. If she came straight out and asked her how old she really was, she'd just upset her. Besides, the teachers and her parents would have put her in the right class!

After a little while, the teacher started writing some science questions on the board. Lucy had always found science tricky because she couldn't remember all the facts and names of things, but Karen seemed to be a genius when it came to science.

When she saw Lucy looking over at her answers, she smiled and told her how she'd figured them out so fast. It was amazing that she could do it so quickly, and it was also great that she was prepared to help Lucy. The tiny girl who never let anything bother her really was making the new girl feel welcome.

When it was snack time, Lucy invited Karen to join her in the playground. They were already getting on so well, and Lucy wanted her to meet all of her other friends.

As they walked over to the group Lucy had known since her first day at school, everyone stopped talking. They looked up at Karen and whispered to one another about how tall she was. Lucy understood how they felt, but she also knew her friends would love Karen when they got to know her.

She told them all about where Karen had moved from, the pets she had at home, and how smart she was with maths and science. Karen smiled and nodded, and before long, another girl asked her what she liked to eat for snacks. They had broken the ice and invited her into their group!

By the end of snack time, everyone had introduced themselves to Karen, shared jokes with her, and heard all about where she used to live. It really was a great day, and one that made Karen smile. She felt right at home, like she had in her old school, and no one cared how tall she was anymore.

When the bell rang, they all went back to their seats, sharing jokes and giggling away. Lucy walked a couple of paces behind the group with a quiet smile on her face. She knew she'd been the one who introduced Karen to the group and made her feel welcome. It was something to be truly proud of.

Karen's first day at school couldn't have gone any better. She'd made many new friends, impressed the teacher with how smart she was, and had made a new best friend in Lucy. As she got into her mum's car, she waved goodbye to Lucy and gave her the biggest smile anyone had ever seen.

When Lucy's parents came to walk her home, they noticed she was smiling to herself and seemed proud of something. When they asked her about her day, they knew their daughter had made someone new feel welcome and they couldn't have been more proud.

Lucy was a brave little girl who never let it bother her how little she was, but she knew not everyone was like that. Karen stood out because she was different and also because she was the new kid in the class. Thanks to Lucy, she'd made a whole new group of friends and really had the chance to get to know everyone.

Do you know the best bit? It all started with the smile and the wave that invited Karen to take a seat beside Lucy. With one little act of kindness, Lucy really had made someone new feel welcome.

Two best friends

It was dark outside, and the rain was hitting the window of Aimee's bedroom. She was worried it meant there was a monster outside that was trying to come in. No matter how hard she tried, she just couldn't get back to sleep.

The next morning, Aimee told her best friend Laura all about what had happened. Laura always slept really well and dreamt about amazing unicorns dancing on rainbows. She hadn't heard the rain or the storm, and she definitely didn't think there was a monster trying to eat Aimee. But she also knew what made her friend happy.

Aimee wanted someone to listen to how she was feeling and understand why she felt that way. She was telling Laura about the monster because she knew she would listen, and that's exactly what Laura did.

Instead of laughing or making fun of her, Laura let her friend say everything she wanted to about her bad sleep. It was a really kind thing to do and made Aimee feel like there was always someone out there who would be on her side.

Before long, Aimee was feeling much better about the monsters. There still might be monsters out there, but she was safe when she was in her bed at home. Her parents would never let a monster in the house, so Aimee felt safe and ready for the best sleep she'd ever had.

That night, the rain came beating down again. Aimee's thoughts turned to the monsters outside. Then she thought about how kind her friend had been and how her parents would always keep her safe. In no time at all, she was asleep and dreaming about playing with all her friends at school. There wasn't a monster anywhere to be seen.

The next day at school, Aimee told Laura all about what had happened. Laura smiled and nodded, then gave her friend a hug. It was a really kind thing to do.

Before long, it was break time and the two best friends were out in the playground to eat their snacks. Yesterday Aimee had been a bit nervous and scared, but today she was bright and bubbly again. But something was about to happen...

Laura looked down and saw a big hairy spider crawling across her lunchbox. She let out the biggest scream anyone had ever heard. It made Aimee jump and look at her friend, but it also made her do something amazing.

She had never been scared of spiders — they weren't her best friends, but she never had a problem chasing them away at home. Laura, on the other hand, was terrified. She looked like she was about to burst into tears and ask to go home. A few of the other kids started to laugh and make fun of Laura. Aimee was different. She remembered how her friend had helped her the day before.

She summoned up all her courage, took a tissue out of her pocket, and reached down and gently picked up the spider. Being careful not to squash his legs, she carried him over to the other side of the playground without saying a word.

Aimee was calm and relaxed, even though inside she was a little worried the spider might jump out! Along the way, she talked to the spider, letting him know she was going to look after him and pop him in a bush where he could eat and have a rest. She got to the bush, opened up the tissue, and let him walk away.

On her way back to where Laura was sitting, she crumpled up the tissue and put it in the bin. She saw her friend was shaking with fear and everyone was looking at her, so she did what any good friend would do and hugged her.

Aimee told Laura everything was okay; the spider was just hungry and now he was far away. Everyone else was making jokes about how the spider was crawling on their backs or running back to get Laura, but Aimee ignored them all.

She held out her hand and asked her friend if she wanted to go inside and do some colouring. Laura smiled and picked up her things. Her nerves were already getting better. By the time they got back to the classroom and had found the colouring pencils, Laura was smiling. It was as if the whole thing had never happened, and when everyone else came in, the jokes soon dried up.

Aimee had done such a great job at calming Laura down and taking her mind off the spider that no one could make jokes anymore. Laura was calm, happy, and smiling, so how could you make a joke about a girl like that?

When Aimee got home, she told her parents all about what had happened, and they started smiling from ear to ear. They knew their little girl had come to the aid of her best friend when she really needed her.

Aimee remembered how kind Laura had been with the monsters before. The two little girls had been kind to each other and that meant they could always ask each other for help. Aimee couldn't have been prouder as she went to sleep.

That night, the rain started hitting her window again, but all Aimee did was roll over and hug her teddy. She knew the monsters wouldn't get in, and she started to think there might not even be any monsters out there at all.

She fell into a deep sleep and dreamt about all the adventures she was going to have with Laura. They really were the best of friends and knew how to help each other when they were scared. Because they were both so kind and brave when the other one needed them, they were going to enjoy a lifetime of adventures together.

That's what being a bright and bubbly little girl is all about.

Henry the adventurous horse

Henry was a clever little horse who was always looking for adventures. He made friends easily and always had bright ideas to share with anyone he met. He also knew how to have fun.

One day, Henry was walking through the woods when he heard a large SNAP! He jumped, clattered his hooves, and then calmed down. What had made him jump?

Henry looked around the woods but couldn't see anyone. When he was just about to give up and carry on walking home, he saw something unexpected. A giant tree had fallen over and loads of broken branches were spread out all over the ground. How could that have happened?

He galloped over and saw that the tree had been poorly. Inside, it looked old and tired, which was why it had fallen over. There was no storm knocking it over and no naughty giant pushing it over. The tree had just got tired and fallen over. What should Henry do now?

When he looked closer, he saw the tree was still big and sturdy; it just looked like it was lying down for a sleep. That meant it was safe for him to play with and bits wouldn't start to fall off it.

Beneath his hooves, he felt the crunch of the leaves and the cracking of the branches. Henry didn't want anyone to trip over them, so he picked them up one by one and put them into a big pile. Before long, he had cleared a path. What should he do next?

Henry didn't want to go home just yet and always had an eye for adventure. He started to think about all the ways he could have fun with the tree and the big pile of leaves and branches he'd made. Soon, he had a bright idea and was busy designing his new den.

He pulled the branches over so they were leaning up against the tree trunk. Henry was quite strong, like all horses are, so he found this bit really easy. Next, he wanted to put a roof on his den using all the leaves and little twigs. But then there was a problem...

As he started to put more leaves onto the branches, the branches started to slip and slide in every direction. There were gaps, there was room for the rain to come in, and soon it didn't look like a new den at all. What could Henry do?

He opened his bag where he had all his arts and crafts things from school — he'd been sent home with some new craft supplies so he could finish his project tonight. He found a big ball of string his teacher had given him. All he had to do was tie the branches together and his den would be nearly complete!

Henry measured the right amount of string, chewed through it, and put the ball back in his bag. He wrapped the string round and round the branches, pulling them tightly as he went. All he had to do now was tie a knot and it would be done. But there was a problem...

Horses like Henry only have hooves — they don't have nimble little fingers and thumbs like boys and girls. How could Henry tie a knot? He knew exactly the person he needed!

He galloped home, across the river and through the fields. Henry was such a quick runner that before long he was at his best friend's front door. She was a little girl called Sarah, and she was very shy, even around Henry.

Henry asked her if she could come and tie a knot for him, but she didn't think she could do it. Henry noticed she was wearing cute little trainers with perfectly tied bows, so he knew she could do it. He just had to make her believe she could.

He told her all about the den, offered to let her ride on his back, and even promised her a big bag of sweets for a job well done. Sarah still didn't think she could do it, but a voice inside her made her want to try. She could do this with her friend by her side; how hard could it be?

Sarah jumped on Henry's back, and they were off! Henry dashed through the fields and galloped across the river faster than he had ever gone before. The girl had never ridden so fast, but the voice inside her kept telling her she could do this. Henry was her best friend and he would have only come to get her if she could really do this.

Once they got back to the big sleeping tree, Sarah jumped off Henry's back and heard all about his amazing plans for the den. He would share it with her. They would tell stories to each other there, and they could even hide snacks there that would be just for them. It sounded amazing!

Sarah picked up the ball of string, smiled from ear to ear, and told Henry exactly what they needed to do. Her nerves had been lost somewhere between the last field they'd crossed and the fence they'd jumped. She told Henry the den would be so much stronger with a branch here, an extra branch there, and a couple of thick twigs in really important places.

Once Henry had put everything in the right place, Sarah took the string, got Henry to pull it tight, and tied the most beautiful bow anyone had ever seen. It was the missing piece of the puzzle that Henry needed to complete the den, and he couldn't have been happier.

They played in the den for hours, sharing stories and trying every type of sweet in the sweet shop. It had all been possible because of

Henry's imagination and kindness, and because of Sarah's courage and willingness to help her friend.

The den would be their special hiding place for years and years, but they never forgot the day they worked together to build it.

Mark the monster chaser

Mark had loved monster stories for as long as he could remember. There were monsters on his walls, on his PJs, and all over his bed. He had cuddly monsters, plastic monsters, and even monsters that made real-life monster noises. His parents thought he would never stop talking about them, which was why they sometimes pretended they hadn't heard him.

Morning, noon, and night, Mark talked about all the monsters he had spotted that day. There were big ones, hairy ones, smelly ones, and thousands of other ones. Each one had a name and a place they hid, and each one had something that would scare them away.

Sometimes, they'd be scared by food; other times, they had to be splashed with water. But, most common of all, they had to be chased away by Mark. He was a monster chaser after all!

One night, Mark was busy lining up his cuddly monsters along the side of his bed. They went from little to large, with the biggest one getting a cuddle from Mark that would last until morning. It was what he loved to do, and it was what made him happy.

Mark's mum came in, kissed him goodnight, and turned out the light. He was asleep before his head hit the pillow, dreaming about all his monster-chasing adventures. But that night would be a little different...

Halfway through the night, Mark woke up. He never normally woke up, and he didn't know why he'd woken up then. He didn't need the toilet, he wasn't hungry, and he never went to bed thirsty. It was probably just one of those things, so he laid back down and tried to get back off to sleep.

But this time, he wasn't asleep when his head hit the pillow. He was tossing and turning, trying to get comfortable. Once he got comfortable, he lay awake for what seemed like hours, but he checked his alarm clock and it had only been ten minutes.

He was about to fall asleep when he heard a rustling sound. That was strange because he didn't have any wrapping paper left over from his birthday — his dad had thrown it all away. Try as he might, he couldn't get to sleep, and the rustling kept coming and going. It was driving Mark mad.

He couldn't figure out where it was coming from because every time he got out of bed, the rustling got quieter. Aha! It must be coming from under the bed! But why would it be under the bed?

Mark didn't keep any toys under there, he didn't keep any clothes under there, and he definitely didn't put anything that rustled under there. What on earth could it be?

He got out of bed, curious as can be, and heard a big sneeze. Could it be a real-life monster? Mark had a look under his bed and saw a tuft of pink fur and some big, green eyes. What on earth was it?

Mark let out a giant roar just like he did when he saw his make-believe monsters, but this time the monster didn't run away. All Mark heard was a little yelp and the sound of big wet tears hitting the floor. Surely a monster wouldn't cry?

That was when Mark knew something was wrong. He reached into his bedside table and found a bag of sweets. He took the sweetest one he could find and rolled it under the bed. Before long, he heard some sniffing and then saw a pink furry paw reach out and take it. Then he heard some really loud chomping and munching, followed by the biggest burp he had ever heard.

He asked the monster if she was okay, but she wouldn't speak to him. Mark really wanted to meet her, so he rolled a couple more sweets under the bed. The same pink paw came out and grabbed them. Soon, the sobbing had stopped and he could sense that the monster wanted to come out, but he also knew she didn't want to be scared.

Mark lay on the floor and looked the monster right in the eye. She looked scared and pulled away, pushing herself up against the wall. Then Mark used his cute little smile to show the monster he wanted to be friends, and her eyes lit up. She knew Mark wasn't going to chase her away.

As she crawled out from under the bed, he was amazed at how small she was. All the monsters he'd pretended to chase away were huge, but she only came up to his waist. As he reached out to give her a cuddle, she held out a little present and gave it to him.

The monster asked Mark to open it. Inside, he found a solid gold medal. It was shining in the moonlight and was the most amazing thing he had ever seen. The monster reached up and put it around his neck. He was the *#1 Monster Chaser*! Mark was so proud that a real-life monster had heard about him and come all this way to give him such an amazing gift. It really did make him feel special and show him that he could do anything he wanted to. But why had the monster come all this way?

As Mark smiled down at her, she began to smile back, slowly at first, but then she burst with delight. She had heard all about the brave little boy who could chase away any type of monster and wanted to reward him. The only problem was, so did all the other monsters.

They were all big and scary and she was just small and nervous. But she was also the only monster Mark wouldn't roar at and scare away. The monsters had picked her because they knew she was the bravest monster deep down, even if she was nervous.

Thanks to her courage and Mark's kindness, she'd been able to give him the medal and make someone special feel even more special. It was a lovely end to a very long day.

A story all about kindness

Alex and Grace were two little girls who always did the right thing. They loved to spend time with each other, loved to tell each other stories, and always loved to eat lots and lots of sweets. They also loved to do the right thing because it made them feel good and helped others around them. This is a story about how they helped many people in one day and made lots of people smile.

When the sunshine started coming through the window, they both woke up from the sleepover. Alex was at Grace's house and they had fallen asleep in the big bed together. All night long, they had been reading stories and talking about their next adventures, but they also wanted to find out new ways to make people smile.

When they went down for breakfast, they saw that there was only enough for one bowl of cereal. They both loved that chocolate cereal so much, so what were they going to do? They could fight over it. They could try to be the first to get it and munch it all down. Or they could share it. Because they always did the right thing, they each had half a bowl of cereal and a big piece of toast. They couldn't have been happier.

As they started getting ready to go out and play in the park, they saw that it was raining. What would they do? They could stay inside and be bored. They could go out and get soaking wet. Or they could take their coats with them. They picked up their coats. Alex found Grace's hat, and Grace found Alex's gloves. They were working together as a team because they loved doing the right thing.

They went out the door and waved goodbye to Grace's parents, then went down the road. They were holding hands, jumping in the puddles, and having a jolly old time. Along the way, they had to cross a lot of roads with cars whizzing left and right. They worked together to look left and right, and they only crossed when they were both happy. Because they were holding hands, they never left each other behind and always felt safe. They truly were doing the right thing.

Before they knew it, they were at the park and ready to play on the swings. There were two swings, but they were both soaking wet. Their parents had told them not to get their trousers wet; just their coats and their boots. They didn't know what to do until Alex came up with an idea. She told Grace that if they picked up a swing together and shook it, all the rainwater would run off. They could only find enough strength to lift it if they worked together.

They picked it up, gave it a big shake, and then did exactly the same to the other swing. Soon, they had two lovely dry swings, and they were ready to play. But there was a problem. They needed someone to push them, and their parents were wrapped up warm at home.

Just like best friends do, they realised that they could each take turns pushing the swing. That meant they could each have a go on the swing and each enjoy a big smile because they were making someone else smile. It was a lovely way to enjoy the park when there was no one else out to play.

Soon, they were getting hungry, so they decided to go to the sweet shop. Grace didn't have any money, but Alex had two pound coins given to her by her parents. She could buy anything she wanted in there, and she was getting really excited.

Just before she was about to pay, she noticed Grace was standing there looking very shy. She didn't have anything in her hands and she looked like she was going to cry. Alex realised that Grace had come out without any money. She didn't have to think twice. She put half of her stuff back on the shelves and handed over one of her coins. That is what friends are for. She smiled from ear to ear and gave her friend the biggest hug when they got outside.

They stopped on a bench and shared all their sweets with each other.

As they walked home, hand-in-hand, they helped each other across the roads, helped each other dodge the really deep puddles, and pointed out the best puddles to splash in. They really were doing the right thing by helping each other every step of the way.

They knocked on the door, went inside, and then took off their wet coats and boots. Grace hung up their coats so they could dry, while Alex put their boots on the radiator so they could dry too. Together, they were helping each other out and making life so much easier.

When Grace's parents asked them how the day had been, they were greeted by two smiling little girls. They knew they were raising the kindest, sweetest little children they had ever seen. Then it was time for dinner.

They were all having fish and chips and Grace's dad came to the door with a big bag that you could smell from the moment he walked in. It was delicious! Inside there were sausages, chips, fish, and a few sweet treats. The girls couldn't have been happier.

When Alex asked if she could have a sausage to go with her fish and chips, she saw that there wasn't enough for everyone. Before she could say anything else, Grace cut her sausage in half and gave half to Alex. Without saying anything, Alex cut off a big piece of her fish and popped it on Grace's plate.

They truly were the best of friends who always did the right thing.

The really excited fish

There once was a really excited fish who never stopped swimming. He had the most beautiful gold scales and shimmered in the sunlight, but he never stood still long enough for anyone to take a good look at him.

From the moment he woke up to the moment he had to go to bed, he would be swimming in every direction. He was a ball of energy who never stopped moving and who always had time to have fun. Along the way, he would get into all sorts of adventures that made him smile and gave him memories he would always love.

When he woke up one Monday, he decided he was going to go to a different part of the lake and see what was happening. He put on his rucksack and set off on his way. He kept taking detours and looking at new things, but he got there in the end.

As he got ready to take a closer look at the mysterious part of the lake he had never been to, he saw another fish he knew from school. She was much slower than him and always took her time. She was bright, funny, and clever, and she also loved to do things slowly. He never understood why she wouldn't want to swim everywhere at once, but he liked her all the same.

When he went over to say hi, he was whizzing in circles around her head, but she didn't move at all. She just gave him a big smile and offered to show him around the lake. She was a bit older than him, so she knew about places he'd never been to. But she said she could only take him if he slowed down. He had to take his time so that he didn't miss anything.

At first, he thought this sounded boring because life was all about having fun, and having fun meant being really fast. But somehow, she persuaded him to slow down and follow her. Sometimes, he would get excited and dash off, but she just kept swimming slowly, going in exactly the right direction. Before long, he would see he had left her behind and dash back to be by her side.

It wasn't long before he realised that he could see so many more things in the lake if he went slowly. His friend was amazing at finding brand-new places he'd never been to, so he followed her right by her side. When he got tired, she still had lots of energy. She told him it was because she always went slowly.

When it was getting dark and it was time for dinner, he asked her how far away his house was. He couldn't believe it when she told him they were just around the corner. This part of the lake looked totally different from anything he'd ever seen, but it was right next to his house. How could that be?

He didn't think about it much and then went inside to have his dinner. When his mum asked him what he had been up to, she was amazed when he said that he had been swimming slowly. For years, she'd been telling him to slow down and enjoy everything around him, but he never listened. Why was he doing it now?

His mum realised that the girl fish had told him things in a way he could really understand. The girl fish didn't mind that he was always moving, but she did want him to slow down and enjoy things. Rather than telling him he was being naughty, or that he just had to do it, she had shown him what would happen if he listened.

It wasn't always easy, because he sometimes dashed off and nearly got lost; but the girl fish kept going in the same direction, nice and slowly. She was letting him see a new way of having fun. Because she was showing him how it worked instead of telling him off, he understood so much better. It made him happy and made him want to share his new way of exploring the lake with his friends.

As he swam through the gates to school the next day, he was really excited to share all the amazing things he'd learnt. His friends had known about them all along because they always swam a little slower than he did, but they still listened.

They were his friends, and they were happy for him, so they heard all about the amazing things he'd found and smiled and made jokes. When he'd finished talking, they each gave him a sweet to congratulate him and make him feel proud.

And what about the girl fish?

She was happy that she'd helped someone enjoy themselves in a completely new way. The secret to what she had done was kindness. She had taken the time to get to know the little fish, and she hadn't let the differences annoy her. Instead, she had enjoyed his company and decided to do something that would make him smile.

When she told her parents all about it, she knew they were listening. They always listened to her, just as she always listened to them. Together, they had lots of fun and it was all based on being kind to one another. Kindness was like a superpower that helped them make new friends, see new places, and enjoy everything.

The next time she saw her really excited little friend, she saw he was excited in a completely different way. He swam calmly beside her and told her all about the amazing things he had found in the lake, and about how they were so close to his house he couldn't believe it. She knew she had made him happy with nothing but patience and kindness. It was a lovely day.

Alice the anteater

Alice loved to eat ants because she was an anteater. Eating ants was what she did better than anyone, and she spent all day doing it. Because the ants were so small and so hard to find, it took a very long time for her to find enough food to fill her big tummy. But she loved doing it, so she never stopped trying.

One day, she found an anthill that was really quiet. She put her big nose inside and tried to find a few ants to eat, but no one was in there. How strange! She had expected to find thousands of ants in there, all trying to run away.

She felt a gentle tickling feeling on her back. When she pricked up her ears, she heard a tiny voice. It was one of the ants, and he was trying to talk to her. He was trying to tell her that the ants were so thirsty and they'd been looking for water for days. They had found a little lake, but they were so small that it would take too long for them to carry enough water back.

He wanted to know if Alice would help, even though she loved to eat ants. She thought that was a crazy idea. Why would she ever want to help him when he was so tasty? But then he told her that he could help her too. He knew anteaters got itchy backs, but it was hard for them to reach. Sometimes, nothing would help. If she helped him carry the water back to the anthill, he would climb on her back and give her a good scratch whenever she needed it. She just had to promise to not eat any of the ants from his anthill.

After plenty of thinking and a little bit of head-scratching, Alice thought it was worth a try. The offer from the ant seemed so unusual and she still didn't really know what to think about it. She did, however, know that she had an itchy back. She asked if the ant could give her a scratch, and he wandered over to the itchy part and got to work. Within seconds, she felt better and had a smile on her face. He had trusted her, so she should trust the ant.

He rode on her back and directed her to the water they had found. It only took her a minute to get there, but she saw how it would have taken an ant all day. She asked him how much water he needed and how often she would have to bring the water back. It sounded like a lot of work, especially when she wouldn't get any food. Alice had to move around all day looking for ants, so she couldn't spend so much time with just one anthill where she had nothing to eat.

At that moment, the ant came up with an idea! He realised that Alice could dig a little track between the lake and a hole by the anthill. It was a little downhill, so the water would gradually trickle and fill up the waterhole right by the anthill. It was such a big job that even a million ants could never do it, but Alice could!

It was a lot more work than carrying back the water, but it would mean she'd never have to carry back the water again. Alice trusted the ant because he'd been kind and scratched her back before he'd even got the help he needed. She got to work digging with her big feet, and by the time night came the waterhole by the anthill was full. She was tired and hungry, but she also had 1,000 new friends.

They climbed onto her back and scrubbed her clean from all the dust and dirt. They even found some tasty snacks in the anthill that she'd never tried before. They were delicious! She couldn't believe how her search for food had turned out today. It was a truly lovely moment.

The next day, Alice was looking for another anthill. She found a strange one which seemed to be hanging from a tree. She'd never seen anything quite like it, but she could hear the same buzz of excitement coming from inside. Or at least she thought she could! She couldn't reach it, so she ran into the tree and pushed really hard. After a couple of attempts, the anthill fell to the ground so she could eat the tasty ants inside.

As soon as she walked closer, she let out a big screech and was in real pain. She hadn't found an anthill at all; she had found a beehive! The bees were buzzing around her, stinging all over her back; she had never been in so much pain. She ran away as quickly as she could and got away from the bees.

She tried to lie down in the dirt to soothe the pain, but it didn't help. Then she tried to bathe in the river, but again it didn't help. She didn't know what to do. That was when she remembered her friends from yesterday.

When she knocked on the door of the anthill, her new friends could see that something was wrong. They climbed on her back and rubbed some medicine into her skin. The pain started to ease, and her smile came back. She saw how important it is to help someone and how it can help you make new friends.

The ants saw how the smallest people can make the biggest difference to anyone in the world. They were proud to have been able to help their giant new friend, and soon they were all laughing and joking.

A girl and her magical bandage

When anyone fell down and hurt their knee, they always knew who to call. Claire was a clever little girl with a magical bandage that would help everyone who used it. It never got dirty, it was always clean, and she took it everywhere with her. She could have kept it all to herself, but she wasn't like that. Claire loved to help people, and that was why people loved Claire.

As Claire was on her way to play football, she saw a little boy fall down and hurt his elbow. It looked really sore, so she walked over to him and offered to help. The boy was crying and didn't want to talk to her, but Claire knew she had to help him. He might get poorly if no one cleaned his elbow, and he would keep crying if no one went to him.

Claire didn't do anything that she thought might upset people. That was why she walked over and sat next to the boy without saying a word. When he started to look at her, she put her arm around him and gave him a cuddle. Before long, he stopped crying.

When he was feeling calm and brave, she told him all about the magical bandage. He listened excitedly about how it would make him better in an instant. He thought it sounded like magic, but people had always told him magic was all made up. He wanted to see it for himself, so he let Claire put the bandage on his elbow.

A weird tingling sensation that felt like a thousand tickles went up his arm. When Claire pulled the bandage off seconds later, his elbow looked as good as new. It was magic after all! The bandage had done something no doctor could ever have done. He was so happy and couldn't believe his eyes.

The next day, Claire saw a man who had hit his head. He was grumpy and quite angry. There was already a big lump on his head, and it was really sore. He needed to get to work, but he couldn't go if his head was hurting. He was annoyed, so Claire sat with him until he calmed down.

She started to tell him all about her magical bandage. He looked at it with amazement as it seemed to shimmer in every colour imaginable. One moment it was a rainbow and the next it was like a shooting star. She put it on his head, and before he knew it, his lump was gone and his headache had faded away. He was amazed and thanked Claire with the biggest hug she'd ever had. When he asked her what he could buy her from the shop to say thank you, she said he didn't need to get her a thing. The good feeling she got from helping him was all she needed.

That night, Claire woke up suddenly. She normally slept right through the night, so it was a real surprise to be awake after dark. At the end of the bed, there was a big wizard who wanted to talk to her. Claire was amazed because she thought that the only magic in the world was in her magical bandage. That was when the wizard told her something that would amaze her...

She listened with wonder as he told her how her kindness had been rewarded with a magical bandage to allow her to help even more people. He told her how her kindness was like a superpower. She then realised that was why she'd been given the magical bandage in the first place. It could only go to someone who was kind and generous and would love to use it to help other people.

Claire was using the bandage the right way because she wasn't doing it to be popular or to show off. She was just using the bandage to help those who needed it most. She felt good about helping people, which was all the reward she ever needed. She also knew that if she was kind to everyone she met, the world would treat her with kindness when she needed something, too.

When Claire woke up in the morning, she told her parents all about the visit. They were delighted. They knew they had raised the kindest, sweetest little girl in the world. Claire was always helping people, and they knew someone had seen the good she was doing in the world.

As Claire walked out the door to go to school, her parents gave her the biggest hug ever. She then crossed the road and found a dog with a sore paw. Without even having to think about it, she reached out to the dog, gave him a treat to calm him down, and then wrapped her magic bandage around his paw. In seconds, he stopped barking and started smiling. His paw was better, and he jumped up to give her a big hug.

As she continued on her way to school, she noticed that the dog was still following her. She turned around and asked him if he was okay, and he said he wanted to help her too. There was a big road coming up that he knew a lot of the children were scared about crossing without their parents. He could see that Claire was getting nervous even when he talked about it, so he stayed with her and helped her get from one side to the other.

Simply by helping the dog without him having to ask, Claire had earned a favour from the dog. He knew she was a good person, so she didn't have to ask for help crossing the road.

Claire kept helping people with her magical bandage, and people kept helping Claire without her ever having to ask. Kindness followed her everywhere she went, and it felt like magic!

The girl who shouted loudest

Charlotte was a little girl who never made much noise. Everywhere she went, she was small and quiet, so much so that most people never even knew she was there. She was quiet in school, she was quiet at home, and she was always quiet with her friends. People liked her because she was sweet and kind, but they never expected her to make much noise.

In school, she would sit quietly and do her work, always listening to what the teacher said. The teachers loved Charlotte because she always tried hard, but they did wish she would start talking a little more. She was so clever and funny that it seemed like a shame she hardly made a sound. Over time, though, everyone got used to how quiet Charlotte was and let her be as quiet as she wanted.

When a new boy joined the class, a lot of the other children made fun of him. He was different from the other kids. He came from a different part of the country, he wore different clothes, and he liked to eat different snacks. Even though he was such a nice boy with lots of stories to tell, the other children just wanted to make fun of him. Charlotte sat quietly and didn't say anything.

When everyone went outside at lunchtime, she saw that the boy was feeling quite sad. Because Charlotte was so quiet, she didn't say anything, but she knew it wasn't right. She took her bag and her snacks and went out to play with her friends.

After a few minutes, the boy came out. The other boys started kicking a ball at him and laughing. Charlotte could see that the boy was going to cry, but what could a quiet little girl like her do about it? She was starting to think about how the boy must feel. He must have been so excited to come to a new school and make new friends, but people had made jokes about him and been mean to him. The boy must have felt really sad, and that just wasn't fair.

Now that Charlotte knew how he felt, she decided to go up to the boy, but she couldn't get close to him. The other boys were in her way and kept making jokes about him. He was going to cry and Charlotte could tell he wanted his mum. Charlotte knew that wasn't right, so she decided to do something she'd never done before.

She took the biggest breath she'd ever taken and let out the biggest roar anyone had ever heard. They were so surprised they stopped talking straight away and looked around at the tiny, quiet little girl who never said a thing. No one expected it from Charlotte, so they couldn't believe it.

Even though she was quiet, she wasn't shy, which meant she had always been able to make friends. The other children in the playground wondered what she was doing!

She told the naughty boys how nasty they were being to the new boy. She asked them how they would feel if a group of boys did the same thing to them. Then she asked them to think about how the boy must feel going through all this alone in a completely new school. A couple of the boys went red and looked down at the floor. A few of them pretended like they weren't involved and tried to walk away. The others just said sorry to the boy straight away.

The new boy looked at Charlotte and gave her a smile. She smiled back, knowing she'd found the courage to stand up for someone who needed it. When they went back to class, she moved places so she could sit next to the boy. He had been sitting alone all morning. She asked him about his hobbies, where he was from, and what he thought about his new school. She found he was funny and clever and could tell jokes no one in school had heard before.

While the rest of the class and even the teacher were talking about how loud Charlotte suddenly became, she was busy talking to the boy. They became friends, and soon everyone else wanted to get to know him too. Rather than talking and not letting him tell his own jokes, Charlotte sat and listened as he made the rest of the class laugh.

Charlotte knew she could be loud when she needed to, but that didn't mean she had to be loud all the time. Charlotte didn't want attention by constantly being loud; she just wanted to use her loud voice to help someone who needed it.

When the school day finished, the new boy invited Charlotte back to his house for tea. Charlotte was delighted that she had made a new friend, and they sat together every day until the holidays. He was funny and always telling jokes, and Charlotte was a little quieter and always laughing and listening. Together, they got the best marks in all of the school projects, acted in the school play, and played together after school every day.

Charlotte could have stayed quiet and just watched that day when the boys were kicking the ball at him, but she didn't. She found a big, loud voice inside of her and had the courage to say something. The boy always thanked her for it and Charlotte was always proud of it. It just goes to show how the smallest, quietest person can do something no one ever expects.

Disclaimer

This book contains opinions and ideas of the author and is meant to teach the reader informative and helpful knowledge while due care should be taken by the user in the application of the information provided. The instructions and strategies are possibly not right for every reader and there is no guarantee that they work for everyone. Using this book and implementing the information/recipes therein contained is explicitly your own responsibility and risk. This work with all its contents, does not guarantee correctness, completion, quality or correctness of the provided information. Misinformation or misprints cannot be completely eliminated.

Printed in Great Britain
by Amazon